# Where the Dark Streets Go

# Where the Dark Streets Go

DOROTHY
SALISBURY
DAVIS

CHARLES SCRIBNER'S SONS · NEW YORK

Davis

# 1 ◆ ◆ ◆

Father McMahon was leaning out the window of the rectory study when he saw the boy in the distance. A little fellow, he was running with all his might in a crazy zigzag fashion, dodging cars and ashcans, a pile of junk and a cluster of women. When he came closer the priest recognized him, and at the moment he recognized him he realized he had found his way into Sunday's sermon: brotherhood was a matter of getting close enough to recognize one another. Since for over an hour he had been at the desk sorting banalities like a curate his shoes to see which pair was the least run down, he sat on the window ledge, swung his legs out and dropped to the sidewalk below. It was spring and the slow rain of early morning had left the smell of earth behind it, earth and the river smell which told of the tide's turning and provoked his memory of the sea's edge and the sand's whiteness, and himself the stranger running there in what once he had thought of as self-pursuit. Always he identified with runners.

He braced himself and spread his arms. "Hold it, Carlos. Slow down."

The youngster crashed into him. When the priest had steadied him on his feet the boy caught his hand and pulled at him. "Come, Father, quick. My friend, the man, he is hurt very bad."

"You can tell me on the way." The priest set his pace by the boy's, his long stride one to the boy's three steps. "Did he send for a priest?"

"No, Father, *si*." Carlos often mixed yes and no as well as his languages. He was growing up bilingual in New York, or, as the monsignor said dryly of the rapidly increasing minority among his parishioners, semilingual.

3

"Are the police there, Carlos?" he asked as they approached Tenth Avenue.

"No, Father. Nobody."

That, the priest thought, would be strange indeed in the crowded tenement where Carlos lived. But the boy led the way, racing against a change in the traffic light and the bursting surge of trucks and taxis. Down a block he ran, then west again to a building marked for demolition, the great white X's scarring the windows. The whole long street, beyond and on both sides, was a desolation. The bulldozers had leveled the rubble to a prairie flatness. The boy led him down three steps and through a basement entry. How he had come to know the man was there, God only knew. The passageway was dank, bile-green, and piled with molding rubbish.

Carlos stopped at a half-open door. "In there, Father."

The priest heard the man's breathing before he saw him, the rattling sound of it all too familiar. The man lay, face down, on a heap of old clothes and bedding. The broken window overhead fronted on the street. McMahon glimpsed the top of a passing truck. He looked around for the boy to instruct him, but Carlos had vanished. He called out his name.

His own voice came faintly back, and then, as he approached the man and knelt beside him, he heard the child pass beneath the window. "Bring your mother, Carlos!" he called to him.

"If you can find your mother, Carlos," the man said with a clarity the priest had not expected.

"Where are you hurt, my friend?"

"As deep as the knife could reach." The man tried to raise his head. His breathing was easier. "Who are you?"

"A friend. I'm a priest."

"Who? Not what." The man rested his head on the back of his hand, the long fingers spread and glistening with spittle. In the gray light his gray face with its glaring eyes and dark beard resembled a medieval Christus.

4

"Joseph McMahon," the priest said. "Shall I go for a doctor if you don't want a priest?"

"It's as late for one as the other, wouldn't you say?"

"You are alive, man. It's not that late."

"Ah-h-h . . ." The sound trailed off. He tried to clear his throat of the rasp starting there again. "You've heard the noise of death in your business."

"Too many times," the priest said.

"I can't get it out of my throat. Come down where I can see you. Turn your face to the light." He lifted his free hand and let it fall in the patch of daylight out of which he then dragged it like something separately alive, a haunting hand, the priest thought, the long fingers squared at the tips. The man clutched it in against himself.

McMahon lay down on the cold cement, flat on his stomach, his face toward the window within a foot or so of the dying man's. He could smell the taint of death. The whites of the man's eyes shone as he tried to focus them on the priest's face. "I think I would like to know you, Joseph McMahon."

"Tell me what I can do to help you."

"Get rid of the pain. Can you do that?"

"I would if I could, God knows."

"Then talk to me. Talk to me of anything but death. What were you doing when the child came for you?"

It was like tunneling out of a dream, going back that little time ago when he had been sitting at the study desk. "I was trying to write a sermon."

"Oh, God almighty. I'm glad I got you away from that."

McMahon laughed. He could not help it, and he was glad, for he saw that it pleased the man. "I would like to know you too, my friend."

"Is it so?"

"It is so."

The eyes slid away from the priest's face, staring past him. When he tried to speak the bloody spittle bubbled up to his

5

lips. McMahon wiped it away with his own handkerchief. The man said, "Nim said once I'd shake hands with the devil."

"Is that what I am to you?"

"No, no, I was only remembering. Do you believe in him, horns, tail and all?"

"I believe in evil, call it what you will."

"So do I, friend. Oh, yes. So do I."

"Do you want to tell me what happened to you?" the priest asked gently.

"No. And I don't want you telling me what is going to happen to me."

"I wouldn't presume to."

"Forgive me, but you are a priest. Do you believe what you wrote in that sermon?"

"I try to write what I believe."

"Are you sure it's not the other way around?"

McMahon had the feeling of dream again, the self-aware dream where you know you are dreaming and so let things go that you might otherwise hold back. "No. I am not sure."

The man showed his teeth in a smile that became a grimace. He burrowed his face in his arm. His whole body shivered with every tearing breath. McMahon stroked the back of his head. He could think of no other comfort to offer, and he could not fortify even himself with prayer.

"You ought to tell me," he tried again.

The man turned his head. "Why? So you could save his soul?"

"Just to take the knife away from him."

"I think I've taken the knife . . ." He cradled his head again in the crook of his arm, the face buried. The shoulders grew still, the breathing stopped.

McMahon heard the scraping of his own shoes as he got to his knees. He knelt on, looking down at the remnant of mortality, an existence no longer, a man who had, the instant before, left off being himself to himself, being. Into your hands,

O Lord, I commend his spirit. He commends his spirit. The priest lingered still and listened to the deep silence of the cellar, the deeper seeming because of the far noises of the city, the *ack-ack* of a pneumatic drill, the thump of the demolition sledge, the deep-throated horn of a docking liner. He got to his feet and went out.

The sunlight was a shock to his eyes. He looked down. The words "Love Power" were scrawled on the sidewalk.

At the first call box on Tenth Avenue he telephoned the police. Then, because he was so instructed, he started back toward the building to await their arrival. He found himself almost greedily aware of life on that little journey: oranges in a basket were like so many suns. He picked one up and turned it in his hand. The shopkeeper rushed out and urged him to have it. He shook his head and put it back carefully. Most people knew him, the women in doorways haloed in hair curlers sunning themselves and their infants, storekeepers and cart vendors, the walkers of dogs, even the dogs. They all knew a priest for a priest if not for a man. A strange thought that, wherever it came from. Then he remembered: *Who? Not what.*

He asked among the women on the stoop of the walkup where Carlos lived if any of them had seen the boy. No one had.

"What did he do, Father?" Their eagerness to hear of mischief was implicit.

"Nothing, nothing. He is a good boy."

"*Si,* they are all good boys," an old one said, wagging her head.

"His mother, she is not home so much," another offered, trying to detain him with the suggestion of gossip.

McMahon walked on. *If you can find your mother, Carlos:* did that mean the dead man knew her? The police would gather and sift the gossip and shake out bits of truth. He heard the first siren as he turned the corner. Waiting, staring at the rubbled field, he caught sight of two doors leaned together like a tent with a tiny flag hoisted atop one end. That would be the first place to look for Carlos.

Detective Finley Brogan took McMahon's statement while they sat in the back of a squad car outside the building. The whole area was being cordoned off, for the crowd came quickly at the siren's wail. Technical trucks, a mobile generator, an ambulance, and car after car of police and detectives converged. Nor were they all investigative. Any incident could fuse the neighborhood, a mixture of blacks and whites, Puerto Rican, Italian and Irish. Volatile, combustible.

Brogan was a well-mannered young detective brought up with a proper respect for the clergy. He asked every question as though it might encroach on the privacy of the confessional. Not so Lieutenant Traynor. When he climbed into the car with them Brogan proposed to read him the priest's statement.

Traynor said, "I don't think it would tire Father McMahon to go over it again. Would it, Father?" His smile was quick to come and go, a weapon of sorts. He was a man of around McMahon's age, forty, lean and scrubbed-looking, with slate-gray eyes. The name was an old one in the parish records.

When McMahon had told the story again, Traynor asked: "Did he come for you, or would any priest have done?"

"Any priest. I happened to be the one at hand." It crossed his mind that the dialogue between the dying man and either of the other two curates would have been quite different. To say nothing of how the monsignor would have dealt with the situation.

"You've never seen him around the neighborhood?"

"Not to my knowledge, but he would have looked different under other circumstances."

"A beard is a beard," Traynor said.

"I got the impression the boy knew him."

"What other impressions did you get, Father?"

8

McMahon hesitated. They were numerous, but he would have to sort them out, to think about them.

"Did he know his killer, for example?"

"He might have."

"Did you ask him?"

"It's there in the notes," McMahon said, pointing to the report book in Brogan's hands. "I asked him if he wanted to tell me what happened to him."

"You were real delicate with him, Father. Because he wasn't a Catholic?"

McMahon felt the prickle of temper. "I'd have been as delicate with a Catholic."

"And him on the point of death?"

Both the questions and answers were wrong, almost the reverse, McMahon thought, of what either of them wanted to say.

"He did not want my advice," he said, trying to end the matter.

Traynor grunted. "There's a girl's name in there some place. No message for her?"

"Lieutenant, I have told as closely as I remember what was said. He gave me no sense of urgency on his behalf, no message, no regret, none of the things we feel should concern a man who knows he is about to die."

"Then why do you suppose he sent the child for you?"

"I'm not sure he did. It may have been Carlos' own idea."

"Then what was the kid doing there?"

"We'll have to ask him that."

Traynor thought about it, his eyes meanwhile sharp to the coming and going of his men. An unmarked car sirened its way alongside them. "The glamour boys," Traynor grumbled, and opened the door to get out. It was only later that McMahon learned he meant the Homicide Division. To Brogan he said: "Pick the youngster up," and then to McMahon: "Puerto Rican?"

"Yes."

"Black or white?"

"White." McMahon did not say it, but Carlos' sisters looked Negroid.

"I grew up in this neighborhood," Traynor said. "But it was a different place then. St. Peter's church. Is that your parish, Father?"

"Yes."

"Give my respects to Monsignor Casey. Does the kid speak English?"

"He can manage pretty well when he tries," the priest said.

"Most of them can. That's the whole problem, isn't it?"

McMahon did not think so but he refrained from saying it. Traynor shook hands with the men Brogan then identified to the priest as Homicide. He and McMahon got out the other side of the car.

"I could use your help with the youngster, Father."

To avoid the following eyes of the curious, McMahon walked the detective to Tenth Avenue. He pointed out the building where Carlos lived, the stoop now deserted. The detective made a note of the address. "It's only a hunch where we're going," the priest said, "but we'll find him one place or another."

"Do you speak Spanish, Father?"

"Well, I don't suppose a Spaniard would call it that."

Brogan grinned. "I'd have the same trouble with an Englishman."

"You don't live in the parish, do you, Brogan?"

"No, Father. In Chelsea, what's left of that. My old man is a longshoreman. Same as Traynor's, only his father's a big *macher* in the union."

"A good English word," McMahon said.

The boy did not come out of his shelter until McMahon leaned down and drew aside the canvas flap which had been tacked on the dirty green doors. The canvas itself was smeared with paint. No child of Carlos' age could have put the play fort together. He came out on all fours when he saw it was the priest.

"This is a friend of mine, Detective Brogan. Carlos Morales."

Brogan stuck out his hand but the child did not take it. Brogan admired the fort, but still won no favor. The boy looked only at the ground.

"Did your friend build it for you?" McMahon asked.

"*Si,* Father. Him and my brother."

"Are they friends?"

"*Si.*"

Brogan reached for his report book and then thought the better of it.

"When did they build it?"

"For my saint's day."

"What's your friend's name?"

The boy shrugged.

"What do you call him?"

"*Amigo.*"

McMahon and Brogan exchanged glances. The detective shrugged.

"Do you know where he lives?" the priest asked.

"In my house."

McMahon put the next question as carefully as he could. "Did you often visit him in the place you took me this morning?"

"Never." Finally the boy looked up at him. "I just go to the steps and call him. He comes down and gives me doorknobs. Would you like to see, Father?"

"I would."

While the boy went into the shelter, Brogan said, "You're doing fine, Father. We'll put it together afterwards."

Carlos hauled out a dogfood carton in which were a dozen or so doorknobs that had once been white but were now painted, some with faces, some like psychedelic Easter eggs.

"Oh, man," McMahon said, "aren't they something."

"Beautiful," Brogan said.

The boy grinned. "Every day when I come from school, he gives me one. If I say what I learned in school."

"Carlos only goes to school in the morning," McMahon explained to Brogan, which in no way explained why he was not in school that morning.

"This week I start afternoons, Father."

"So you went early to see your friend?"

Brogan shook his head. He did not like the prompting.

The boy said, "Yes, Father. Only he did not come when I call. I call again. Then he call me. 'I am hurt, Carlos,' and he tell me to come in the basement. I want to run away, but he say, 'Please, Carlos.' So I go in. He was like this." The boy humped over, hugging his hands to his chest. "He say, 'Don't be afraid,' but I am afraid when I see the blood. And when he fall down and don't talk any more I come for you."

"Carlos, do you remember the first time you ever saw the man, the first time?"

"*Si*, Father. He was painting Mrs. Phelan's door. He let me paint too."

Brogan asked his first question: "Did you see anyone else in the building where your friend was hurt?"

The boy glanced at the priest.

"Tell him," McMahon said.

"No."

"Not ever?"

The boy shook his head.

"You're a good boy, Carlos," the priest said. "Better put your doorknobs away now."

About to go into the hut, the boy saw the crowd for the first time. He looked up at the priest.

"I'll wait for you," McMahon said. Then to Brogan: "I'll have to tell him."

12

"Thanks a lot, Father. It may not sit with Traynor, but if you'll come round to the station this afternoon, we'll try it on him. Do you know this Mrs. Phelan he mentioned?"

"She owns the building I pointed out to you. She lives on the first floor." He knew Mrs. Phelan very well, but he was not going to say that to the detective.

"Is there a Mr. Phelan?"

"Yes," the priest said tersely.

"Okay, Father," Brogan said after waiting purposely for the priest to go on. "I guess I can find out for myself what that's all about."

McMahon watched the detective take a short cut across the field. "Come, Carlos," he said. "I'll walk you home."

# 2 ◀ ◀ ◀

"Joseph? Father McMahon, you're late for luncheon."

He had hoped to get by the dining-room door without being seen, but the old man was watching for him. He sat like a family scion at the head of his table, and although there were only the two of them present, Father Purdy, the youngest priest of the four attached to the parish, sat in his own place, two chairs down, on the monsignor's left.

"I'll be right in," McMahon said. "I have to clean up a bit."

Miss Lalor, the housekeeper, poked her head out of the kitchen. "Will I set your soup, Father?"

"Not till he's at the table," the monsignor answered for him. "There's nothing worse than a slop of cold soup."

"He'll be in a hurry, Monsignor."

McMahon left them to settle the service of his lunch between them. They had been bickering for over twenty years. Monsignor Casey had brought her from Ireland after the war. That too was a matter on which they contended: whether she should have come or stayed in Galway and married a man with a mule and a garden. She was, by Father McMahon's lights, one of those women destined from the cradle to become a caretaker of priests. She was also one of the best cooks in the archdiocese—the hallway was sweet with the fragrance of her Friday pudding—but since St. Peter's was becoming more and more a poor parish, it was the monsignor's tart pleasure to end most of their arguments by saying it was time he gave her over to someone who could keep her in the style to which she was accustomed. Their relationship was something McMahon sometimes thought about: the naturalness of it, the

14

unnatural made natural somewhere in Ireland generations ago.

Whatever stain it was he had picked up on the basement floor was not going to come out of his clothes with spot remover. He had to change into his other suit. Paint or tar or blood. He sniffed at it: the smell was not strong enough to overcome Miss Lalor's sugar and spice. He was indeed late, he noticed by the clock on top of the piano. So he took another moment and gathered the music on which he had been working the night before, the score to Rachmaninoff's *The Bells*. He had arranged it himself for female voices. It was something the high-school girls could really swing on.

He ran down the steps and laid his briefcase on the hall table. He remembered then the half-written sermon he had left on the study desk and went to the front of the house to get it. *Do you believe what you wrote in that sermon?* I try to write what I believe. *Or is it the other way round?* A devil's advocate could not have attacked more succinctly. He wanted to think about that and about the dead man. Instead he sat down and made a note on brotherhood, the thought that had come into his mind when he recognized the running child. It no longer seemed very original.

Miss Lalor came to the study door. "Father, he's getting into a temper."

"I'm coming." He would as soon have gone without lunch and gained himself a few minutes for thought, but he followed her down the hall and paused only long enough to stuff the sermon into his briefcase.

"Was he a hippie, do you think?" The monsignor loved the word for some reason although he had little use for its designate.

"An old one then," McMahon said. "The police will soon know."

"They're the worst kind. It's a short step from the East Village to the Bowery."

15

"No, I don't think he was that kind."

"A pervert maybe?"

"What makes you say that?"

"The child, the child." The old man was as impatient with the cream jug, pouring the cream with a splash over his pudding.

"It was a healthy relationship, I'm sure."

"Healthy. Never mind was it healthy. Was it moral?"

"That's what I meant," McMahon said.

"Then why don't you say it? I can't stand these quibbling words you young fellows come up with nowadays."

McMahon ate in silence. Father Purdy folded his napkin and asked if he might be excused.

"We haven't upset you?" the monsignor said with an almost mocking tolerance he assumed toward the young priest. Purdy was earnest and easily put down. In his year among them he had not come to understand that the old man's brusqueness was his style and a carefully cultivated one. Purdy flushed when anything harsh or intimate was said in his presence and McMahon suspected that his show of naïveté was a style with him also. His own lack of patience with the boy priest, as he called him, was sometimes close to contempt.

"I have a Christian Doctrine class at one, Monsignor," Purdy said. Which, since the class was actually described as Ecumenism in the new curriculum, did not ingratiate him with McMahon, however the old-fashioned words might please the monsignor.

"Lieutenant Traynor asked to be remembered to you," McMahon said when Purdy had left the table.

"Is that Mike Traynor's son? A lieutenant? I thought he'd go up in a hurry, but not that much of a hurry." The old man sat back in his chair and dabbed his whole face with his napkin. His normally pink complexion always went florid by the end of the meal. "I baptized him . . . No, I suppose not. It's his confirmation I'm remembering. There was the question of the

16

sponsor, one of the labor men his father wanted. I think he was a Communist. An ex-Communist, that was it." He laughed to himself then, remembering. "I can see Mike now, those shaggy brows of his going up." He mimicked the brogue as though he had not a trace of one himself. " 'Father Casey, half our executive are ex-Communists. It was the mixed marriage of the 'thirties.' "

Miss Lalor brought McMahon his pudding.

"Would you put it aside for me and I'll have it later, Miss Lalor. My singing girls will be waiting for me."

She returned to the kitchen, throwing a shoulder block on the swinging door.

Monsignor Casey said: "Is there a tune to it, whatever you're teaching them now, Joseph?"

"Oh, a lively tune, Monsignor," he said and blessed himself and left the table. The question was rote as was his answer, but he never failed to rankle under it, which he supposed was a lack of humility in himself. That the monsignor was proud of the St. Peter's Girls' Choir, he knew. It had some little fame in the archdiocese. The girls had sung for the Holy Father during his visit to New York and every year they gave several interfaith benefit concerts. McMahon was fairly sure that it was his work with them that forestalled his transfer to a larger parish or to one of his own, the latter an assignment he truly did not want.

He sat at the piano improvising softly while the girls filed in, the long and the short, the skinny and the squat, the black and the white, the knock-kneed, the piano-legged. Though they sang with the voices of angels, they came in like a herd of elephants. When Sister Justine had them in their places, he warmed them up with a few minutes of folk rock. He enjoyed the anachronism it made of him in their eyes. He was a stern disciplinarian and his tastes in music were as severe. Yet he loved to shake them loose this way, to set their breasts and buttocks bobbing, all of them letting go. Or almost all of them. Some of them were pretending. There was the sadness, the pretense. To please him? To fit in? It was a kind of self-denial, the kind he did not like, and he caught an image of these pretenders marching into their futures, into marriage, motherhood, or into maidenhood, treading the heels of these very shadows they were casting now before them. He realized that beneath the musings he was thinking of Priscilla Phelan and the marriage he had been trying to mend although he deeply felt it should be dissolved.

He ended with a kind of *Eulenspiegel* fillip. The groans and laments were shut off by the staccato snaps of Sister Justine's frog. The snapper was as familiar to her fingers as the beads of her rosary. He got up from the piano and gave over the bench to sister who would play such notes as he needed to structure the *a cappella*.

"*The Bells,*" he said, while the music was being passed. "We shall work only with sounds today. Forget the words. For most of you that won't be any hardship. All the sopranos: Bell, bell, bell. First altos, bong, bong, bong. Second altos, boom, boom, boom . . ."

Throughout the rehearsal his mind kept going back to the man in the cellar and to the child, Carlos, who took the word of his death as philosophically as the going away of someone he had known, his own father, for example. Carlos' sisters, Anita and Fran, were in the choir, and after practice McMahon detained them and spoke to the elder of the two.

"Did you go home to lunch today, Anita?"

"Yes, Father."

"Was Carlos there?" He had told the boy to remain at home until his sisters came. His mother was away at work.

"Yes, Father. There were policemen. They came looking for Pedrito. Everywhere they looked like he was hiding and they asked us questions."

"What questions?"

Anita looked to her sister for help, but Fran was shy. A homely, awkward girl, she never expected to be called upon, and he wished then that he had addressed her first.

"About where Pedrito worked. What time he went to work. My mother. And about Mr. Muller."

"Mr. Muller," McMahon repeated.

"He was killed with a knife. They asked did Pedrito have a knife. I would not tell them. Pedrito does not like the police. Nobody likes police in our house."

"Did you know Mr. Muller?"

"Yes, Father. He was a very nice man. He came to Carlos' saint's day."

"And he sings songs he makes up for Carlos, for my mother so she laugh, for everybody." This was Fran. Muller had obviously been able to draw even her out.

"You both liked him, did you?"

The girls nodded.

Anita said, "The police, they want to know who did not like him. And Mrs. Vargas tell them, Mr. Phelan. She don't like Mr. Phelan, you see, Father. Otherwise, she don't tell anything."

McMahon did not like gathering gossip from the girls. Nor did he want to make them late for their next class. "Did you take Carlos to school this afternoon?"

"Yes, Father. He don't want to go, but we make him go. Otherwise . . ." Anita gave herself an uninhibited slap on the rump by way of illustration.

# 3 ◆ ◆ ◆

McMahon finished his sermon when he got back to the rectory. He did not like it at all now: brotherhood and closeness, a sentimental myth. He found himself testing each phrase in the light of the dying man's challenge, and he wanted to cross out more of what he had written than he wanted to retain. He was annoyed with himself. Or with the dead man? See here, he wanted to say, perfection is a luxury. But faith is a greater luxury. Where the latter thought had come from he did not know. He had provided his antagonist with dialogue. Perfection should be a goal, and to a priest faith was a necessity. The only marks he put on the paper in the end were the dashes with which he always marked his breathing places, and while he tested these, his mind slipped comfortably off to the parish priest of his childhood, upstate, who seemed not to take a breath from the first word to the last of his sermon. At the breakfast table after the eight o'clock Mass when Father Dunne had preached, the family would piece together what it was he had said. McMahon could remember now his father's saying: "It may seem like a great joke, but stop and think about this: you'll remember years from now some of the things we've figured out here at the table, and some of the mission priests with their fire and brimstone you'll forget forever." And it was true: many a sermon he had himself built on a few words caught from Father Dunne's whirlwind.

Monsignor Casey came to the study door. "Mrs. Phelan is in the parlor asking to see you. She says it's important."

"She might have phoned first," McMahon said. His eyes went to the window as though in search of escape.

20

"Let me talk to her then. I'm an old man with some of my troubles past me, thank God."

Which could only mean, McMahon thought, that he had taken the measure of Priscilla Phelan. "I'll go, I'll go," he said.

He saw a difference in the woman the minute he walked into the room. Her red hair was drawn back and bound in a clasp behind her head where normally she let it go, a wild mane she tossed from around her face while she talked. Nor had she made up her face in the usual way, her eyes shadowed wells, her lips a wounded pucker. Now, wearing no makeup at all, she revealed herself a woman with good natural features, and he wondered which face she wore for Phelan, trying to coax him into her bed, for this was the problem about which she had been coming to him off and on for several weeks.

"You ought to have called before you came," he said.

She made no apology. Nor did she bat her eyes or go through any of the phony posturing that had so put him off her. He had suspected from the beginning that she came to him because he was the best-looking priest she could find. There were times during their sessions when he thought she was getting sexual enjoyment out of describing to him her husband's hangups. "Father, I've lied to you."

"Well," he said, looking down at her, his arms folded, "you're not the first person who has lied to me, and I don't suppose I'm the first person you have lied to."

"That's true, Father. I've also lied to Dan."

"To your husband." He said the words to curtail the intimacy implicit in the use of the name instead of the relationship, man and wife.

"I've been with another man."

"For how long?"

"Several times."

"Over how long a period?"

"Two weeks or so. Please, Father, don't keep looking at me. If I came to you in the confessional you wouldn't."

21

"It was your choice of where you came to me, Mrs. Phelan," he said, but he went to the window. In their previous conversations it had taken an act of will on his part not to flee her eyes. "When were you here last?"

"Wednesday night."

"Why did you come if you knew you were going to lie to me?"

"I still wanted to help Dan . . . my husband."

McMahon tried to remember how their conversation had gone on Wednesday night. He could not sort it out from their previous meetings. "I don't quite understand that," he said.

She got up and with a stride the very self-assurance of which he could feel disarming him, walked to the parlor door and closed it. She came and stood beside him. "It's your fault I'm in this mess, Father McMahon. I don't mean you did anything on purpose. God forbid! But the more we talked, it made me wild. Is that a sin? I can't help it. It's the way I'm made, that's all."

"You should not have come to me then," he said. "There are other priests in the parish." He retreated to the little table with the Donnegal shawl over it, angry with her, angrier with himself. He was sure she still was not telling the truth. But that she was trying to tell it now, he had to admit and to deal with. "Or better—most women in your position would have gone to someone in another parish entirely."

"Most women wouldn't go to the priest at all. They'd be ashamed. I like being a woman. I like what I feel." The color had come into her cheeks, a color that made the eyes eloquent as no makeup could.

For the first time he felt a sincere compassion. Perversely, this enabled him to deal with her more severely. "Sit down here at the table and listen to me for a minute." He waited and then seated himself opposite her. "Let's try to be honest with one another. Why did you come to me? Let's dispose of that first."

"Because I thought, he's a priest who would understand."

22

"Is that the whole truth of it?"

She rested her elbow on the table, her hand, scrubbed clean and without the nail polish, at her cheek so that briefly he was reminded of the hand of the dying man—just in the sensitive use of it. "I'm pretty well educated, Father. I read a lot. There's a bar I used to go with Dan to. Now I go alone when he goes off on his own, promoting some scheme or other, God knows. I sit there and talk with people I've got a feeling for, people who can't get where they want to go. I mean they want to be writers, they're taking polls on the telephone. They're painters . . ." She made a gesture as though to brush the hair away from her face forgetting that she had fastened it at the back. "I forget what I started to say."

"Why you came to me in the first place."

"Because you're a musician."

McMahon felt both stunned and humbled.

"Oh, that isn't the whole truth either. Who knows the whole truth about anything, about anybody including yourself? Myself, I mean. I told you the first time I came to see you that I loved Dan, that I wanted him. I know, you don't want to hear that again." Her eyes had caught his in flight.

"You are wrong," he said. She was not wrong: he could feel himself tensing against the repetition of futile intimacies, but he said what he thought was now necessary. "If that's the way you can get at the problem, tell it again."

"No, I won't. I won't talk about Dan. I think I know now what I was doing here though I didn't mean to at first, I was trying to get you going. But that was because I needed to know if I could. Can you understand that?"

"I think so," he said quietly.

"You're a funny one, you know. I got the idea you liked it."

"That was an unwarranted assumption," he said and stared her down. Many a female he had stared down, but most of them were adolescent schoolgirls and easily frightened out of —or into—their fantasies.

"The man I was with is dead," she said flatly.

McMahon let the words rest in silence. He had expected them. What silenced him within himself was that both he and Priscilla Phelan had talked these few minutes as though the death had not occurred.

"The police came. I went with them and identified him as the person I'd rented a back room to. I gave them my extra key. Do I have to tell them, Father? They'll be asking. About me and him, I mean."

"You will have to judge its relevance."

"It's not only me—it might hurt Dan."

He refrained from saying that she should have thought of that earlier. "In what way? Does your husband know of the relationship?"

"I'm not sure, Father. He could have been guessing. When I stopped trying to do what you told me to do . . ."

"Helping him make love to you," McMahon said out.

She nodded. "When I stopped all that—when I just lay there like a whore last night, that turned him on." She broke then, open as even she had never been and spewed out the bitterness. "When I didn't want him he was like a bull. Christ, Father! What's the matter with us?"

"Something I don't think I'm capable of healing," McMahon said. "Maybe, just maybe, it will heal itself—your marriage, given a chance now. It's much too simple for me to say. And I could have been wrong in counseling you the way I did. By trying to provoke his manhood, you may have been taking it away from him."

"It sure is simple that way, Father. But what's inside me isn't simple any more. It's closed up like this." She clenched her fist.

"Time, time," he said, "and prayer. That's the greatest opener I know."

"Maybe for you. For me it's like sucking my thumb. Or something else I won't go into now. It makes me forget for a while, but it doesn't settle anything."

"You said Dan suspected the affair you were having with this man."

24

She smiled a little and sounded almost wistful. "You make it sound so important."

"Wasn't it important to you at the time?"

"No, Father. I'm sorry, but I'm trying to tell you the truth. You want even sin to be romantic."

"Especially sin," he snapped to cover his chagrin that she should mock him.

"It wasn't love. It was just plain sex. I seduced him. You won't have any trouble believing that, will you? You know, most of the tenants in my building don't buy this business of going to the priest every time somebody gets into somebody else's bed. They talk about it on the stoop, in the kitchen. It's the way they are. Maybe that's why I can live with them.

"Last night after Dan got through proving himself, he got up and dressed again. He said to me, 'Now you got something new to tell your friends.' 'I don't tell them anything,' I said. 'That's not the message I get from them.' 'Then they're lying,' I said. 'Are they, Pris? About the bearded gentleman in the back room? Who is he? What is he?' 'He's a man,' I shouted and Dan said, 'So now you have two men, lucky girl.' He went out then, Father, and I haven't seen him since."

"Have you told any of this to the police?" McMahon said after a moment.

"Not much, except about Dan not being home. They'll start asking. It was mostly Gus they wanted to know about."

"Your husband has been away overnight before, hasn't he? If a job took him out of town?"

"Yes, but he's not on one now."

McMahon yielded then to an impulse he had been trying to repress. "Tell me something about the man—Muller."

"He was murdered this morning in that condemned building on the other side of Tenth Avenue."

"I know. I was with him when he died. Carlos Morales came and got me."

She thought about that. "Now I understand. Carlos . . . He loved kids. I wouldn't be surprised if he's got some of his

25

own somewhere. He'd make nice babies with the right woman. A gentle person . . . but *with* it." She was silent for a moment, her eyes thoughtful. McMahon waited. He knew quite a lot about her, some things she wanted him to know and some he had learned by inadvertence. He knew that she was thirty-two, the daughter of a broken marriage who had spent her childhood and adolescence in a convent boarding school, and then, when her father died, her mother had brought her home to live with her in the tenement building she now owned herself: a clash of environments if he had ever known one. She and Phelan had been married when she was nineteen and pregnant for the first and last time. The child had been stillborn.

"It's funny, Father," she went on finally, "but I can't talk about him that way, me, the big talker."

"But you said it wasn't important," he chided gently.

"I guess it was just that I didn't want it to be important. I liked him a lot. I don't even think Gus Muller was his right name. Gust—I always forgot the 't' and he liked it. We met in the Duminy Bar I told you about on Ninth Avenue. He needed a room cheap and a job he wouldn't have to pay taxes on. So we settled on him painting the apartment." She looked at her hands where she had clasped them tightly on the table. "I slept with him that night. That sounds pretty raw, doesn't it, Father?"

"Since you say it yourself," he murmured. "What else? What did he do before he started drifting?"

She shook her head. "He wouldn't tell me. 'I am who you think I am. That's all you need to know. And when we're together, it's all I need to know.' And the funny thing is, he was right. I didn't care who he was. We were like two people cut loose in space, only I wasn't afraid."

"And yet you came to me Wednesday night and pretended you were still trying to help your husband."

"I wasn't pretending. I'd made up my mind—for Dan's

26

sake—to keep on trying even if I didn't care any more."

"Have you any idea what Muller was doing in the building where he died?"

"No. I used to hear him go out very early in the morning—dawn. He'd work for me in the afternoons—and other places. He'd come home sometimes walking along with Carlos or carrying him on his shoulders. Home . . . a shirt, a razor, a toothbrush, and a pair of clean shorts hung up to dry on the back of the chair."

"If the women gossiped to your husband they will to the police too, you know."

"No. You're wrong about that too, Father. They wouldn't tell the police the time of day. It's up to me what I tell them. Me and Dan."

It was she who was wrong: one of her neighbors had already told the police that Phelan did not like Muller.

"They're bound to ask questions," he said, "the man living in your house."

"It's a back room, separate. Its own door. The john's in the hall."

They were both avoiding the real question, Phelan's capacity for violence. McMahon made up his mind he would not be the one to bring it into the open. "You ought to go home and wait for your husband."

"What if he doesn't come home? The police will want to know why."

"Could you tell them why?"

"No, but . . ."

"I'd just leave it at no, Mrs. Phelan."

"I will, but they won't, Father. Dan has an assault record. He cut up a man with a bottle once."

"Over you?"

"Hell, no," she said bitterly. "Over a dog that lifted his leg on Dan's shoe."

# 4 ◆ ◆ ◆

At five minutes past five McMahon approached the precinct headquarters. He noticed that one of the two white globes that hung on either side of the entrance had been smashed. It was odd, the association, but he thought of the words, "Love Power," scratched on the sidewalk outside the doomed building. Not so odd. One was as sure a sign of the times as the other. He also saw Carlos and his mother before they saw him. Mrs. Morales gave the boy a push out the door ahead of her, but then, seeing the priest on the steps, she caught her son's curly head and hugged him against her. Carlos responded as limply to affection as he did to abuse.

"He's a good boy, Father, but sometimes I don't know what to do with him." When she spoke the gold of her teeth glittered.

The priest ruffled the boy's hair with his hand.

"His brother, he is the bad one." She jerked her head toward the station, which indicated that the older boy was in now with the police. "He hates the police. Why? They have a job to do like everybody else. He would like them to beat him, that's how much he hates them. He was the same with his father. I do not understand. If you speak to him, Father, tell him, please, to be more polite?" The pleading of her voice was as ancient as motherhood.

"I will," McMahon said. What he did not say was that Pedrito Morales had little more regard for priests than he did for the police. Or his own father. But she knew that too. The conversation was its own kind of ritual, not entirely false, but the forms barely holding together.

At the bottom of the steps she turned and called after him: "Father, he was a good man, Mr. Muller. Everybody wants he

28

should have a nice funeral. You know?" By the rubbing to-
gether of her fingers she suggested money. "Come to my house,
Father. The people liked him. They will all give something."
That, he felt, was genuine.

He asked for Brogan at the desk. The sergeant directed him
to a room on the second floor. He went up by way of a staircase,
the color and smell of which put him in mind of a cheap hotel.
The windows were wire-meshed on the outside, sealing in the
dirt of generations. He met Brogan and Lieutenant Traynor
coming out of the room with Pedrito, a tall, skinny boy of
eighteen, sallow and sullen, with a mop of black hair and a
scraggle of beard.

The best he could do for him at the moment was to ac-
knowledge an acquaintanceship. "Hello, Pedrito."

The boy nodded curtly.

"Keep your nose clean, young fellow. We'll be watching
you," Traynor said.

"*Cochinos*," Pedrito snarled. Pigs. But by then he had
reached the stairs.

"Makes you want to love them, doesn't it?" Traynor said.
He went on down the hall.

Brogan led the priest into the interrogation room where an
officer was removing the tape from a recorder. They waited
until he had left the room.

"So you had to bring Carlos in anyway," McMahon said.

"*Si*," Brogan said. He searched a folder for the statements he
wanted.

McMahon was not to be put off. "Why?"

Brogan shrugged. "The lieutenant didn't like it, not the
way the kid told it to us. The doorknobs were what really put
him in a flap."

"I don't get it."

"Well, Father, let me put it this way: he questioned the boy
on whether Muller had molested him."

McMahon's temper snapped. "Balls."

"Exactly."

"Christ Jesus help us," McMahon said, but he already knew he was being unreasonable. The luring of a child to an abandoned building: it could be construed that way. Even the monsignor's first question was whether the man was a pervert.

Brogan half-sat on the desk. He indicated the chair to the priest. "What is it that bugs you, Father? You know yourself that a kid like Carlos, there's nothing he's going to learn from us he didn't know from the street already."

McMahon sat down and took in hand his own typed statement. What Brogan said was true: trying to shield the innocence of a child in Carlos' environment was almost as impossible as the restoration of virginity. He read the statement and signed it.

"But you're right," Brogan said. "That wasn't Muller's trouble."

"What was?"

Brogan shrugged. "Mrs. Phelan? Or vice versa. I have a notion she was hot for him. There's gossip in the building. Even we can get to it. She picked him up in a bar, nested him down in her back room. Like charity begins at home. Where was Phelan through all this? Where *is* Phelan?"

And what's his problem? McMahon kept the thought to himself, but he suspected Brogan was doing the same thing. He asked, "Is Pedrito in the clear?"

"As far as the homicide, he has to be. He works on a machine assembly line. Twenty witnesses to where he was from six A.M. to three this afternoon. And he wasn't a chum of the victim. That was Carlos' idea. To a kid, I guess, everybody over fifteen is the same age, especially if they come to his birthday party. They all drank wine that night and it was then Muller got the idea of building a house of doors for the youngster. Pedrito went with him. If he gets into no worse trouble than swiping doors, I'll settle."

30

McMahon said, "Why are you a cop, Brogan?"

The young detective colored. "To stay out of the draft. I'll take my law and order straight, Father."

The priest was not sure why, but he felt a kind of respect for Brogan saying it.

"Phelan has an assault record, by the way," Brogan added.

"Was he at the birthday party too?"

"No, but Mrs. Phelan was."

"It makes you wonder why there was gossip, if she's so popular with her tenants," McMahon said, "and they're not notoriously cooperative with the police, are they?"

"It's pretty simple, Father—it's not the infidelity, if that's what it is. Homicide is something you can get put away for a long time. They don't like Phelan."

That had to be it, McMahon realized. Priscilla Phelan had not calculated the relative values of her Spanish-speaking friends. "Do you want me to go over Carlos' story?"

"It won't be necessary, unless you want to see it. You can go over to the house if you want to—I'll fix it up—if you want to see his things. There's not much there. He was traveling light, wherever he came from. A sign painter by his identification."

McMahon shook his head: he did not want to go near the Phelan apartment.

Brogan tapped his statement with a pencil. "I just thought by this you might be interested."

"I am," McMahon said. "He got to me and I'm not sure why. Was it his courage? He was ready to die, but it was as though that was because he wanted to live, to live right up to and over the threshold. And he said he would like to know me. That always sets a man up, doesn't it?"

"It sure does, Father."

"There was more to him than what he left in that room, I feel pretty sure of that."

"Then have a look at his things."

"No. That's your business. But you're right. I'd like to know."

"I'll keep in touch with you, Father. Thanks for coming in."

It was a good time of day, McMahon thought, reaching the street. Next to dawn he loved it the best, the last hours of the sun when its heat was spent but a golden haze hung over the city. The youngsters were playing stickball, and great fat women leaned out their windows watching for their men to come home from work. There were flags in the windows of almost half the apartments. No college deferments here. Brogan was not a young man whose insight should be underestimated: he would not say to many people in this neighborhood that he joined the force to avoid the army.

Crossing Ninth Avenue he decided to walk downtown a few blocks to Ferguson and Kelly's funeral parlor. It was no new thing to him, trying to arbitrate the costs of a funeral: he generally did well until the family arrived to select the casket. This part of town, where the street markets commenced, was predominantly Italian. Sausages and cheeses hung in the windows over stacked canisters of olive oil, two-quart tins of tomatoes. The produce was all outdoors. The people were noisy and friendly and a priest was accepted as one of themselves, neither feared nor revered. It was a strange place for Ferguson and Kelly, but as he thought about it, he could not name an Italian in the undertaking business. That they left to the morbid Irish. But obviously in Italy Italians buried Italians. Could the circumstance here be the dominance of the Irish in the church? Since Muller was not a Catholic, or so he assumed, he would have to see Ferguson, a man he took to be of Scotch-Irish antecedence. He would rather have negotiated with Kelly. As he opened the door setting off the muted chimes, he wished he had telephoned. A typical McMahonism: taking the